The ABCs of Paradise Found

KAREN AMANDA TOULON

Illustrations by **ERIC RHINEHART**

Foreword by **Andrew Young**, former United Nations Ambassador

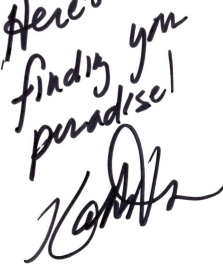

*Dear Leon —
Here's to finding you paradise!
Karen*

The ABCs of Paradise Found

The ABCs of Paradise Found

All rights reserved. Printed in the United States of America.

No part of this book may be used or reproduced in any manner whatsoever without the copyright owners' written permission except for the use of quotations in book reviews.

Illustrations are proprietary and may not be reproduced or used in any way without written permission of the illustrator except for the use in book reviews.

The characters and events portrayed in this book are fictitious. Any similarities to real persons, living or dead, are purely coincidental and not intended by the author.

The ABCs of Paradise Found © 2021 Karen Amanda Toulon and Eric Rhinehart

First Edition

ISBN: 978-1-946274-66-3 (Hardback)
ISBN: 978-1-946274-67-0 (eBook)

LCCN: 2021910368

Front cover design: Omomato

Karen Amanda Toulon's Cover Photograph: Eric Rhinehart

Eric Rhinehart's Cover Photograph: Karen Amanda Toulon

Interior Layout: Amit Dey

Published in the United States by Wordeee Beacon, NY 2021

Website: wordeee.com
Twitter: twitter.com/wordeee
Facebook: Facebook.com/wordeee
E-Mail: contact@wordeee.com

Advance Praise

"Karen Toulon has written a poetic tribute to French Caribbean culture, and the vagaries of new relationships. Eric Rhinehart's paintings invoke the color palette and culture of the islands so well you can swim in them. *The ABCs of Paradise Found* is a lyrical and romantic tribute."
—*June Cross, Fred W. Friendly Professor of Media and Society, Columbia University*

"I found myself absorbed in the unfolding of every letter, anticipating what would come next. This is a beautiful collaboration, a marriage of Karen's intimate personal chronicles and Eric's brush, which capture in each scene a sense of festivity, myth and memories of presence. A gift for those who only know the Caribbean from a distance as well as those who know it like yesterday."
—*Reggie Woolery, Deputy Director for Exhibitions and Programs Artspace New Haven*

"Reading *The ABCs of Paradise Found* feels like a nostalgic afternoon going through your childhood photo albums; this story allows you the space and time to reflect on the specific moments in life that become memories. Fueled with the spirit of the Caribbean, Karen Amanda Toulon's diction and Eric Rhinehart's illustrations harmonize in a beautiful, soothing symphony. Through the alphabet, Toulon gives us a guide to tracking the evolution of this grounded, contemplative meditation on life, relationships, identity, and the passage of time."
—*Phillip Youmans, Filmmaker*

"Like all art, this book is a journey of discovery. With the familiar rhythms of an ABC book and a lush tropical setting, it conveys the mysterious magic of adult love and the wonder of seeing a cherished place through the eyes of a lover. A perfect marriage of image and text, Rhinehart's luminous paintings and Toulon's poetic prose reveal how paradise can be found in a person as well as a place."
—*Mary Birmingham, Curator Visual Arts Center of New Jersey*

"The lagoons and palm-fringed beaches in Karen Amanda Toulon's *The ABCs of Paradise Found* speak of the fluid and sensual rhythms of island culture, mythology, and love. Eric Rhinehart's bespoke illustrations have the influence of many: Gauguin, Bernard, Matisse. With extraordinary craftsmanship, he captures the dazzling beauty of people and places, both seen and unseen, with an expressive visual language of intense color that is uniquely his own."
—*Anthony Liggins, Artist, Gallery 88*

"This book is about a journey—where one person remembers and the other discovers the indigenous beauty of Dominica. The vivid watercolors and alluring prose transport us into a Caribbean Island full of history, culture and mystique that a couple absorbs together, while rediscovering each other along the way."
—*Alexis Clark, Journalist, Author, Enemies in Love: A German POW,*
A Black Nurse, and an Unlikely Romance

"The stories conveyed took me down memory lane growing up on a Caribbean Island. From the vibrant colors, to the layers of colloquial terms used by our ancestors that stirred up such excitement and adventure that you will only experience in Paradise. Thank you for sharing such moments, as a certified island gal, this book will be on my shelf to share with generations to come!"
—*Erin E. Brown, International Spokesperson & Advocate*
University of the Bahamas, Disability & Inclusion

"*The ABCs of Paradise Found* is a delightful read and a visual treat! Part love story, part travel guide, readers are led on a sensory-filled tour of Dominica through this charming adult storybook. Rhinehart's luminous and inviting illustrations wonderfully convey the essence of Toulon's seductive prose."
—*Stephanie James, Director, MW Gallery;*
Curator and Collection Educator, Mott-Warsh Collection

"*The ABCs of Paradise Found* is a mesmerizing, magical journey through the Caribbean. The book's seductive, enchanting words, coupled with its whimsical paintings, tell of memories—real and imagined—in a world of fantastical adventures. It's a refreshing, restorative read perfectly suited for anyone ready to take a flight of fancy."
—*Susan Raphael, Secretary, New York Travel Writers Association*

"*The ABCs of Paradise Found* presents readers with delectable gifts from Toulon's fondest memories and Rhinehart's twenty-six dreamy illustrations in living color from A to Z. Discover myriad rivers and streams, morsels of yellow cake, green bananas, Spanish limes, the magic of an Emerald Pool, dine on Callalou, taste Ti Punch, try on a Wob Dwiyet, dance at Carnival, and much more. The island is Dominica, casually dubbed "The Nature Island of the Caribbean." You'll see why. The book is a joyful romp from yesterday for today, a must read."
—*Michael Zufolo, Producer & Co-Host, LET'S TRAVEL! Radio*

Dedication

To our parents, our daughters, sister, and brothers—
the keepers of our hearts.

Foreword

by

Andrew Young, former United Nations Ambassador

The ability to make connections that take you outside of yourself can help you to better understand, and find joy and purpose in, the world around you.

This is a lesson I first learned within my family and a lesson that was reinforced by my family of friends, teachers, mentors and other supporters. They all offered their guidance and encouragement; they helped me to make connections that have transformed my life and I believe the lives of countless others.

Connections mattered when I was growing up in New Orleans, learning how to navigate my complex community of race, religion, economics and culture. Connections mattered when I attended Dillard and Howard universities and met other driven students, including the father of Eric Rhinehart, illustrator of *The ABCs of Paradise Found*. We lifted each other up to succeed—to see over the horizon— at a time when the prospects for Black people in America remained stubbornly shortsighted. Like my own father, Joe Rhinehart would go on to become a dentist, while I would attend divinity school, and then join Dr. Martin Luther King Jr.'s movement for racial justice.

All of my experiences, working for social, political, and economic justice at home and around the world—as a Georgia Congressman, Mayor of Atlanta and as the U.S. Ambassador to the United Nations—have served to strengthen the importance of investing time to connect, to listen, to share stories, to be open to hearing other people's points of view.

In 2003, I founded the Andrew Young Foundation to support and promote education, health, leadership, and human rights in the United States, Africa, and the Caribbean. *The ABCs of Paradise Found* tells the story of a woman from the Caribbean who is deeply connected to her family, her culture and their link to the history of the African Diaspora. She proudly shares her stories with an outsider, who in turn listens and learns. Through this connection, we see that both are enriched. Her appreciation for some of the simple things in her life—childhood memories and local fruits—grows. And while she reflects, he absorbs her tales and begins to tell stories of his own.

There is power in an open mind and heart.

Introduction

On Finding Paradise

This story is about places that are real, and characters who may be conjured from memories.

It is about events that are true, and those times when truth makes way for dreams and desire.

It is about believing in the supernatural, and being naturally nervous about believing in someone new.

It is about the joy of discovery, and being proud of the paradise that your heart calls home.

Atlantic Ocean

We are at the edge of the Atlantic Ocean. The boisterous bigger cousin of the Caribbean Sea.

I like to think you notice me before I notice you.

"Why isn't anyone going in?" you seem to ask no one.

We were invited separately to a beachside picnic on the Atlantic side of the island.

"You can't take a seabath on this side. The sea can take you," I explain, but then decide to self-translate as I speak. "It isn't safe to swim in the Atlantic. It's too rough. We swim in the Caribbean. On the other side of the island."

You digest my answer as your gaze glides back to the sea.

I survey you as you survey the shoreline.

The sea can take you.

Bwa Kwaib

You want to know what you have been seeing as you make your way around the island.

You describe it for me. It's the flower of this place—its shocking crimson blossoms outshining the sun.

Sturdy, tolerant, long-lasting. It usually hugs the coast, but it can ascend the mountains. Friend to hummingbirds and the yellow-chested bananaquits.

I tell you that it's the *Bwa Kwaib* or Carib Wood. Later you'll look up its official name: *Sabinea carinalis*.

Callalou

We meet for lunch. Your idea. We're having *callalou*. Our national dish. My idea.

Callalou gets its name from the dark green leaves of the dasheen plant. Along with the leaves, a soup pot is loaded with yams, green bananas, dumplings, coconut milk, seasonings, pepper, a bit of smoked pork, and if you're lucky, land crabs. Lots and lots of land crabs. Their pointy edges stick out of the swampy stew like shards of glass.

There really is no delicate way to go about it. I fish a crab leg out of my bowl with my fingers, stick it into my mouth and bite down just hard enough to crack the shell while simultaneously sucking the sweet meat out.

You smile and stick a leg into your mouth. Success.

Dominoes

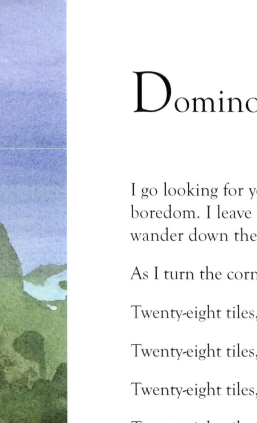

I go looking for you. We are at my friend's home—a small gathering—and I fear I have lost you to boredom. I leave the women falling over in synchronized laughter to a story we've all told before and wander down the veranda.

As I turn the corner, I hear a loud "crack" and I know what has befallen you. The curse of the domino.

Twenty-eight tiles, originally carved from bone.

Twenty-eight tiles, tracing back to China one thousand years ago.

Twenty-eight tiles, catching on in 18th century Italy and then circling the globe.

Twenty-eight tiles, capturing the Caribbean's fancy and never letting go.

There are rules but all I know is that dominoes usually involve surreal amounts of rum and slamming the tiles down on the table with as much punishment as possible.

There you are—looking like a local expert. You glance at me sideways and smile, then turn back to your newest fixation.

Emerald Pool

The Emerald Pool—that's where we've slipped away for a cooling swim.

It reveals itself to us—almost hidden by the rainforest canopy that surrounds its edges and nearly obliterates its part of the sky. Fed by a waterfall, the pool reflects the green and blue of the trees and sky—coloring all emerald.

You stick out your tongue and say you're a snake.

Later we'll try to bake ourselves dry on the surrounding warm rocks like lizards.

Fête

"*Fête*," I say. "We've been invited to a *fête*." Somehow "me" has become "we."

I must admit I am a bit excited.

You want specifics. I am not surprised.

Fête. An elastic word used to describe a party that might swing from a tame *soirée*, where the biggest disgrace might be falling short of ice, to a full-on *bacchanal*—sweaty with sins.

I silently tick through the location, the invited, and the possible unknowns.

Ice will be the least of our worries.

"There will be food and drinks," is all the guidance I choose to offer.

You smile that smile that I am beginning to understand.

Gato

We stop at the bakery to buy cakes for later. There are coconut cakes and pastries filled with guava jam. And *gato*.

"Yellow cake?" you guess.

"No-definitely-not-yellow-cake," I insist. It is weightier. And you can savor the ingredients: the butter, the sugar, the eggs, the flour.

Shopping complete, we head back to the car, where a nibble turns into a feast.

We sit in the hot car cramming chunks of *gato* into our mouths.

Hélé

Hélé. At its simplest, it is a shout. But it really is so much more.

Venture to the Saturday market, and get carried away by the calls of the sellers, compelling you to notice them and only them.

We return from our shopping excursion, loaded with provisions to last a lifetime.

Green bananas

Plantains

Yams

Tannias

Breadfruit

Christophines

Jelly coconuts

Iguana

My cousins had an iguana. Part gecko, part dinosaur. The big cousins used to warn the little cousins not to get too close. Or else.

"Or else?" You don't understand.

"Or else…" Apparently your cousins did not have an iguana so you are having trouble imagining the unimaginable.

"Or else," I measure my words and recite the memory with glee:

"It would lash us with its tail and cut off our feet!"

J'ouvert

I ask you to come out to play at *J'ouvert*. A riff on the French "*jour ouvert*"—open day. *J'ouvert* is the beginning of it all.

It's when Carnival first opens her eyes. When—in the predawn hours—revelers take to the streets to begin the two-day process of singing and dancing away a year's worth of worries. Before Ash Wednesday and the 40 day sobriety of Lent leading up to Easter sets in.

Later in the day there will be full-blast calypso and soca, *sensay*, *bwa-bwa* stilt dancers, and bands of people grouped in organized costumes running *mas* together.

But for now, there are the simple sounds of the *syak-syak* scraper, the *lapo kabwit* goat skin drum, and the *boumboum* boom pipe, mixed with the spectacle of the Pappy Show Wedding— where fantastic homemade couture concoctions rule.

I can make no promises where I will be once the sun comes up. But for now, *J'ouvert* with me.

Kalinago

The *Kalinago* people call this island *Waitukubuli*, meaning "Tall is her body." They are the original residents—here for one thousand years and their ancestors for thousands of years before that.

The *Kalinago* were here before Christopher Columbus and the rest came sailing in with their tall ships, renaming the island and calling her people "Caribs."

The *Kalinago* were here before the slave traders and the land cultivators.

Before the tour operators and experience-seekers.

Before the two of us.

Lougawou

Sitting at dinner with the moon beaming overhead, I am trying to remember a nursery rhyme about night skies, but I give up and instead suggest that we—actually you—might want to be careful walking home.

"Why?"

"*Lougawou*. Werewolf. When there's a full moon, some people can shift themselves into *Lougawou*," I explain. "So you better be careful."

"I better be careful?" You're laughing. "I'm not the one wearing those ridiculous sandals. I can make a run for it."

Morne

"*Morne*" sounds like "moan," you muse half out-loud as we wind our way up one of the countless mountains. *Morne Bruce. Morne Diablotins. Morne Trois Pitons.*

Each twisty-turn seems to exponentially increase the distance between our car and our stolen glimpses of the sea below. Sometimes we gasp together.

Christopher Columbus was less impressed. After landing upon the island in 1493, he returned home and described what he had seen by taking a piece of paper, crumpling it up and throwing it down. Nary a flat surface in sight.

Whether here or anywhere, carved out curvy roads make me nervous, so you are driving.

I look to you for reassurance, but you are rolling "moan, *morne*" around over and over and over in your mouth like the stone of a long-gone fruit. Your road mantra.

I wonder where this will end.

Negres Marrons

Negres Marrons—runaway slaves who battled to overturn the savage system of slavery, their determination finding support in the island's equally defiant terrain.

The thick rainforest mountains provided refuge, where *Morne Negres Marrons* gets its name.

I contemplate how long I can hide without being found.

Old Market

The Old Market was used for centuries to trade commodities—everything from people from Africa to produce from around the Caribbean. Public executions were said to be held here.

Now the cobbled square is where locally made baskets are lined up for tourists' inspection and hats, t-shirts, and madras clothes hang from market stalls.

You pretend to patiently wait while I select the perfect basket to add to my collection.

Parrots

We keep hoping to see a purple and green *Sisserou* parrot but we will have to make do with second-hand accounts.

Usually the *Sisserou*, and its red-necked kin the *Jaco*, live deep among the trees.

My cousin tells us how, after a hurricane stripped its rainforest home to sticks, she was saddened to see *Sisserou* flying low into the villages in search of food.

Qenip

Qenips or Spanish Limes—*Mamoncillo*—are native to South America, pollinating the Caribbean in pre-Columbian times.

The eyeball-sized fruit goes by many names: *qenip, kennip, genip, quenepa, xenipe*...you get the point.

But the feeling when eating one is the same.

"Bite it," I instruct you. "Firmly."

You put a *qenip* between your front teeth and apply just the right amount of pressure to its perfectly round, leathery green skin to result in a productive, almost audible "pop."

Your eyes open wide and you look like someone who has just been caught doing something equally wonderful and wrong.

Your bite exposes luminous, tangerine-colored flesh that is sour, sweet, somewhat like its *lychee* cousin and must be sucked-scrapped off its large center seed with your teeth.

"More," you demand, and I am happy to oblige.

Rivers

Rivers, rivers everywhere. *Indian. Layou. Rosalie. Roseau.* Three hundred and sixty-five.

"One for every day of the year," I boast.

"But is there a complete list, naming them all?" You want to know.

Of course you do.

"You're missing the point," I snap.

I am exasperated. Sometimes you just have to believe.

Soucouyant

I am certain the *Soucouyant* is real; you claim you are unconvinced. But then I catch you looking at the darkening sky with concern, giving me hope.

A reclusive old woman by day, at night the *Soucouyant* strips off her skin, storing it in a mortar, before soaring through the air to seek her prey. The *Soucouyant* greedily feeds off the blood of her human victims while they sleep.

That bruise you can't explain on your thigh or on the meaty part of your upper arm? *Soucouyant*-bite! But she'll meet her end if you put coarse salt or pepper in the mortar; the *Soucouyant* won't be able to put her skin back on!

In the morning you are all smiles—that smile, that smile—as you proudly show me an angry mosquito bite and claim a *Soucouyant* visitation.

Ti Punch

We sip *Ti Punch* as we decide on what to do about dinner.

This *apéritif* borrowed from an island neighbor is all the alchemy that we can manage.

We split the duties like two old-timers:

    2 oz *rhum blanc*

    1 tsp *sirop de canne ou sucre de canne*

    Fine tranche de citron vert avec du zest

Under the Sea

You want to see under the sea. Citing my phobia, we agree you must go without me.

You come back and dazzle me with unbelievable stories of your own.

Stories of Champagne Reef, where bubbling water rises from volcanic thermal springs on the ocean floor, and sea sponges named pink azure, red rope, yellow tube and purple vase make themselves at home.

Valley of Desolation

"No," I tell you, "this really is a place. Not make believe. Past my grandmother's home."

The Valley of Desolation.

There you'll find the Boiling Lake—the world's second largest hot-lake. Bubbling gray-blue-green water, hot enough to boil an egg—courtesy of a direct line to the Earth's core.

The Valley of Desolation.

You can almost hear the remnant weeping of long-gone women taking stock of their lives' losses.

"If I was going to cry, it would not be over losses. It would be because of disappointment," I feel the need to explain, although you did not ask.

You seem to take it well.

Wob Dwiyet

I've brought a formal dress with me, just in case the occasion arises.

I put on my *Wob Dwiyet* for you. You look at me fully and pronounce me beautiful in a whisper.

In another time, the *Wob* was a gown said to be worn by freed slaves on Sundays. First came floral fabrics; later, madras.

My bespoke *Wob* is black and navy, shot through with pewter thread.

You bow to me like we are at court and we do a few silent twirls until the heat overtakes us.

X-Ray

I'm inspecting a jagged scar on your shoulder, which you blame on a motorcycle mishap in your younger years.

"My father had a motorcycle accident when he was young," I say. "He was knocked unconscious."

"...and?" You're drowsy, half listening in the sun.

"And, back then, I don't think the hospital had an x-ray machine so after a few days, they called in a priest to perform an exorcism."

You turn over with a jolt. "A what? An exorcism? Like in the movies?"

"I have no idea what they do in the movies," I say. "What I do know is that they figured an exorcism couldn't hurt so they brought in a Belgian priest. My father woke up to the priest saying, *"Sortez, Satan"*— get out Satan, in French."

I stop talking and look down at you. You are looking up at me, silently grinning.

Finally you say, "I'm glad it worked."

Yenyen

It has come to this. We've fully exposed ourselves. We've swapped family stories, joined the crowds at *J'ouvert*, and survived a *Soucouyant* encounter. I've even inspected your passport photo and realized that at one point in your life, you simply looked deranged.

There is nothing left to explore except to compare words. I say this. You say that.

"*Yenyen* is a good one," I say. You have to say it with a twang.

"*Yen* is...?" You look interested. It is a good one.

"*Yenyen* are like fruit flies. Not mosquitoes. Nets and sprays won't help. They're annoying invisible flies. You can't get away."

I come to regret this lesson as you amuse yourself by calling me "*Yenyen*" for the rest of the day.

Zouk

Zouk music, that distinctive French-Caribbean sound. Gathering up everything with its generous horns and drums—the water, the rum, the mountains, the flowers, the food, the people—and pushing it all back out through the speakers of a place where we have come to dance.

This is our first time together at this place, but I know this has always been our place.

The music has a pulse, but you have your own—slightly off and fully confident.

In the middle of the dance floor, you hold me at arm's length and flash me that smile that I have come to miss when it goes away.

You shout something and I think I hear you say, "How could anyone ever want to disappoint you."

The ABCs of Paradise Found Plates

Page 2
Atlantic Breaking,
Watercolor, 18 in. x 10 in.

Page 5
Bwa Kwaib with Bananaquit,
Watercolor, 18 in. x 12 in.

Page 6
Café du Caraïbes,
Watercolor, 17.5 in. x 11 in.

Page 9
Veranda,
Watercolor, 17 in. x 12 in.

Page 10
Emerald Pool,
Watercolor, 18 in. x 11 in.

Page 13
Garden Party,
Watercolor, 20 in. x 11 in.

Page 14
Highstreet Bake Shop,
Watercolor, 18 in. x 12 in.

Page 17
Market Day,
Watercolor, 20 in. x 12 in.

Page 18

Iguana,

Watercolor, 18 in. x 11 in.

Page 21

J'ouvert,

Watercolor, 21 in. x 14 in.

Page 22

Waitukubuli,

Watercolor, 18 in. x 11 in.

Page 25

Lougawou,

Watercolor, 18 in. x 12 in.

Page 26

Mountain Road,

Watercolor, 18 in. x 10 in.

Page 29

Escape,

Watercolor, 20 in. x 13 in.

Page 30

Old Market,

Watercolor, 11 in. x 9.5 in.

Page 33

Sisserou,

Watercolor, 17 in. x 10 in.

Page 34

Qenip,

Watercolor, 17 in. x 9 in.

Page 37

Indian River,

Watercolor, 20 in. x 11 in.

Page 38

Night Visitor,

Watercolor, 19 in. x 14 in.

Page 41

Petite Rum Punch,

Watercolor, 17 in. x 11 in.

Page 42

Below the Surface,

Watercolor, 21 in. x 11 in.

Page 45

Valley of Desolation,

Watercolor, 16 in. x 10 in.

Page 46

Lady in Waiting,

Watercolor, 19 in. x 12 in.

Page 49

Possession,

Watercolor, 18 in. x 12.5 in.

Page 50
Swarmed,
Watercolor, 20 in. x 12 in.

Page 53
Danse Zouk,
Watercolor, 20 in. x 11 in.

Acknowledgements

We would like to thank former UN Ambassador Andrew Young for his thoughtful words, as well as all of our early manuscript readers—who offered cheerful criticism, endless encouragement and kind comments.

We are grateful for our family and friends who fill our memories and make us whole.

And we are humbled by the legacy of strength, creativity and grace of those who lived and loved on lands near and far so we could be here today.

Karen Amanda Toulon and Eric Rhinehart